GREEK TALES
THE BOY WHO CRIED HORSE

Bloomsbury Education
An imprint of Bloomsbury Publishing Plc

50 Bedford Square
London
WC1B 3DP
UK

1385 Broadway
New York
NY 10018
USA

www.bloomsbury.com

First published in 2007 by A&C Black, an imprint of Bloomsbury Publishing Plc
This paperback edition published in 2017

Copyright © Terry Deary, 2007, 2017
Illustrations copyright © Helen Flook, 2007
Cover illustration copyright © James de la Rue, 2017

A catalogue record for this book is available from the British Library.

ISBN
PB: 978 1 4729 4201 2
epub: 978 1 4729 5281 3
epdf: 978 1 4729 5282 0

2 4 6 8 10 9 7 5 3 1

Typeset by Newgen Knowledge Works (P) Ltd., Chennai, India
Printed and bound in UK by CPI Group (UK) ltd, Croydon CR0 4YY

To find out more about our authors and books visit www.bloomsbury.com. Here you will find extracts,
author interviews, details of forthcoming events and the option to sign up for our newsletters.

TERRY DEARY

GREEK TALES

THE BOY WHO CRIED HORSE

Inside illustrations by Helen Flook

BLOOMSBURY EDUCATION
AN IMPRINT OF BLOOMSBURY

LONDON OXFORD NEW YORK NEW DELHI SYDNEY

INTRODUCTION

Troy, 1180 BCE

Aesop the Greek storyteller said: *There is no believing a liar, even when he speaks the truth.*

I live in an invisible city. The city of Troy. Once, the finest city in the world. It's not there now. It's gone. The wind blows across the plains and covers the stones with sand and dust.

'How can this be?' you ask. 'How could a mighty city turn to a crumbling ruin in my lifetime?'

I will tell you, if you will listen. Troy would still be there now if they had listened to me back then. The trouble was, I told lies.

But I'm not lying now.

You believe me, don't you? I am Acheron the Liar. The last Trojan. And this is my story. Listen and learn...

CHAPTER 1

My mother used to tell me stories.

"I'll not forget the day you were born," she'd say. "The day our brave Prince Paris came to Troy. He stood upon the palace steps and spoke."

Then Mother would stand and raise her chin. Her eyes would gaze into the distance and she became our prince. "People Trojan, greet you I with deep joy, godly thanks give us for journey safely homeward be today in shiply sail."

"Why does he speak like that?" I'd ask.

Mother would shake her head. "Our Paris is good with a sword. Hopeless with words. He tangles them up like wet washing on a windy day."

And then she'd tell me how Prince Paris showed the Trojans his new wife, Queen Helen. "Lovelier than a great steak pie," she'd sigh.

When you are starving every day, then *nothing* is lovelier than a great steak pie. We were lucky to get a little rat meat in our watery soup.

The trouble was, Prince Paris had *stolen* Queen Helen from the Greeks. And no sooner had he landed back in Troy than the Greeks arrived...

"We want her back!" her husband, Menelaus, said. "We'll stay right here, outside your walls, until you starve to death."

"Not a chancely hopeful thing, think I," Prince Paris laughed. "We overstuffy with foodlets!"

"And that happened the day you were born," my mother said. "Ten hungry years later, and still we battle on."

In the palace, Prince Paris found ways to feed the people. Troy was a huge city with

many little gates to sneak food in. A deep
well in the market place made sure that we
had water.

The best food went to Paris and Helen, and the next best to the fighting men who stood guard on Troy's massive walls.

The next best went to the people working in the palace. The rest of us were left to live on scraps – or any rats that we could catch.

But soon even the rats were as thin as the east wind that blew across the plains of Troy.

And that was why I learned to be a storyteller.

Every Friday, they had a feast at the palace. They ate proper pies with tender goat or dog meat and gorgeous greasy gravy. Poets sang stories of the heroes and were paid with a pie.

I learned to write poems and sing them
to Paris and Helen. Long story poems that
went on for half a feast.

Of course, the tales I told were lies. I
made Paris and the Trojan heroes sound
like gods because that's what they wanted

to hear. I made the Greeks appear as weak as the seaweed on the shores where their ships rested.

So I am a liar. If you were hungry, then you'd lie, too.

CHAPTER 2

That Friday evening was the last evening
Troy would ever see.
It was the evening
I met the stranger.
I met him on the
road to the palace.
He was an old man
with a grey beard
and a dusty robe.
He slipped from the
shadow of a side
street and stopped
me. He pointed at
the tortoise shell
I carried. "You have

a lyre," he said. "You must be a poet."

"I am. I'm going to sing for Paris and Helen at the palace."

"Then I'll come along with you," he said. "You can show me the way."

"Everyone knows where the palace is," I said.

23

"I am a stranger," he told me.

I walked a few paces over the paved road, and then stopped. "There are no strangers in Troy. The city has been locked for ten years to keep out the Greeks. How did you get in?"

"There are ways," he said softly. "Lead on. Perhaps you can help me get inside the palace. I need to speak to Paris."

"Why should I help you?"

"I'll give you all the food you ever dreamed of... and more," he promised.

I said I'd lie to help him. If you were hungry then you'd lie, too. I didn't know I'd betray my city, did I?

We walked on through the moonlit streets to the palace. The wind from the plains seemed to shake the moon and pushed us up the hill. The guards knew me well and let me through. "Who's this?"

they asked and pointed at the man.

"My dad," I lied. My dad had died fighting
in the first few weeks of the war. I'd never

known him. I always thought he'd be like this kind-eyed, grey-haired old man.

The palace hall was bustling with servants and guards, magicians and jugglers, dancers and musicians. I knew them all.

Torches flamed and crackled along the walls. A trumpet blasted out a tuneless fanfare*.

"Ooops! Sorry – a few wrong notes in there!" the trumpeter grinned. "I proudly present my Lord Paris and his Lady Helen!"

* I'm a singer. I hate bad music. Sorry, but it has to be said: the trumpeter should have been shot with a poisoned arrow.

The people clapped politely and Paris entered. He was followed by the sly-eyed, sour-mouthed Helen. (That's what my mother says now.)

Paris raised a hand. "Commencify us the juggly and the musi-magic singerly songerly entertainables!"

The stranger muttered in my ear, "What is he saying?"

"Don't know," I shrugged. "It's all Greek to me."

We watched the dancers snake and sway, and a magician who made a duck appear from Helen's hat.

Then it was my turn. But as I stepped forward with my lyre, the stranger pushed me aside. He bowed before Paris.

"Whattalie wantable?" Paris asked.

"News," the stranger said. "I bring great news!"

CHAPTER 3

"My name," the stranger said, "is Sinon, and I come from the Greek camp."

Helen jumped to her feet. "A Greek? In Troy? Kill him, guards! Kill him!"

There was a swish of swords as the guards marched forwards but Sinon raised a hand. "I hate the Greeks!" he cried. "They are cowards on the battlefield. Mighty Paris here is greater than *ten* Greek warriors!"

"It's truthly rightable," Paris said.

"What I came to tell you," Sinon went on, "is that the Greeks are running away."

"*Away?*" Helen said and her sly eyes squinted at the old man.

"Back to Greece. They say they have been here too long. That they have more important things to do. Other wars to fight. They have sailed off in their ships and left behind a mighty wooden statue to remember their heroes!"

"They *have* no heroes," Helen sneered.

"Not herolic like Paris princelet!" Paris laughed.

"Their statue will stand on the windy plain of Troy for all the world to see," Sinon said softly. "Every ship that passes will see it and remember the Greek heroes."

"*Statue*?" Helen asked. "What is this statue? A statue of some hated hero like Achilles?"

"Paris princelet arrowed Achilleres in the heel-o and deaded him dead with tippy point poison*!" Paris cried.

"It is the statue of a horse," Sinon said. "You can see it from the city walls. Maybe it is

* That was true. Paris was too much of a coward to face the great Greek Achilles in battle. He shot him from behind with a poison arrow. Of course, I didn't sing *that* story in my poems!

a gift from the Greeks to noble Paris. It will stand there and remind you of them every day."

"No it won't!" Helen roared.
"It won't?" Sinon said.

"No. We will bring it into the city and use it for firewood. We will not let passing ships see anything Greek," she raged. "Paris... give the order!"

"Ahem!" Paris cleared his throat. "Statute horsling insideify Troylum getter sunshiny day."

The guards stood still. "What did he say?" one asked.

Helen sighed and explained. "Tomorrow at first light we'll drag the wooden horse inside the city."

"That'll be hard work. We'll need lots of pies to give us strength," a guard grumbled.

"Now the Greeks have gone w
go hungry again. You'll have pies
and pies every day of your life!
promised.

Of course she didn't know their
from that night on would be short.
short. Very, very short.

CHAPTER 4

The feast began before I could sing my new poem. I saw Sinon the stranger slip out of the palace hall, and I followed him. I would return and sing for my pie after

the feast. Sinon said he was a Greek who hated Greeks... but he didn't say why. I didn't trust the man.

The stranger hurried back down the moonlit hill to the spot where he'd met me. He turned into a bat-black alley and headed for the north wall. I followed and watched.

A guard stood by the wall and waved a spear at Sinon. "Who goes there?"

"Sinon the Greek-hater," the old man said. "You let me in. Now let me out."

"You promised me a pig's head if I let you in," the guard said.

"I'm off to get it now. The Greeks left lots of food behind."

The guard nodded. He pushed at a stone and part of the wall slid open. Sinon patted his arm and walked out onto the moon-silver plain.

I ran to the gate.

"Acheron the singer!" the guard cried.

"Shush, Cottus!" I hissed. "Let me out. I'm following that man."

"Don't you go pinching any pigs' heads those Greeks left behind. The first one is mine."

"You already have a pig's head on your shoulders," I muttered and pushed through the gap in the wall.

Sinon was plodding over the plain. The Greek tents were gone, but ashes from dead fires and broken swords of dead men showed where they had been. I kept to the path around the edge of the plain and ran in the shadows of boulders.

We were close to the shore now and the moon was blocked by a huge shape. The shape of a wooden horse, almost as tall as the walls of Troy.

Sinon waved to the horse as he walked past it. At the water's edge, there was a wooden pier that the Greeks had built.

A single ship stood waiting and Sinon walked towards it. The east wind carried the voices to me:

"Is it done, Sinon?"

"It is done. They take the horse in tomorrow morning."

"That's when we will return."

A rope was untied and the ship was rowed out into the wind-chopped sea.

It was a mystery. Sinon had said they were gone for good, so why were they talking of returning?

I wandered back over the plain towards Troy and looked up at the horse. On the moonlit side, I saw something I hadn't seen on my way out to the shore.

A rope ladder hung down the side. I heard voices of men and they seemed to be coming from within. I heard the rattle of their armour and swords as they moved around.

Then I understood. And I knew what I had to do.

I sped over the silver-sanded plain and back to the walls of Troy. I called for Cottus to open the gate. "Did you see that old feller with my pig's head?" he asked as the stone swung open. "I want it on a plate."

"It'll be *your* head on a plate tomorrow if you don't let me through. Quickly! I have to warn Prince Paris!"

I ran over the cobbles until my bare feet were stinging, and up the hill until my lungs were burning. I burst into the feast and cried, "Beware of the wooden horse!"

CHAPTER 5

"A singerly songerly!" Paris cried when he saw me. The wine jars were all empty now and the royal faces were as red as a Trojan sunrise... the last sunrise Troy would ever see. Even the guards were drunk.

"The Greeks are planning a trick!"

"Singerly songerly!" Paris roared and banged the table with his knife handle.

"He wants you to give us one of your poems, Acheron," Helen cried. "Do it!"

"But..."

"Do it or we will be eating *you* in a pie at the next feast," she snarled.

I'd lost my lyre. I had no song. I had to make it up as I went along. I began:

"The Greeks they left a gift, a wooden horse;

It isn't all it seems, you know... of course!

The horse is stuffed with soldiers, fully armed.

Once they're inside our walls, they'll do us harm.

Just leave the horse out there upon the plain,

Or Troy will die and never rise again!"

Helen picked up a knife and threw it at me. I ducked and it slithered over the marble floor. "That is the worst poem I've ever heard. You should die for that!"

"But it's the truth!" I wailed.

"Acheron, you are a poet and a storyteller. It is your job to tell us *lies* – tales about how brave Paris is, when we all know that really he's a weedy little coward."

"Cowardy whobee? Songerlees of bravebold Paris trulyful is!" Paris tried to say.

"You, Acheron, wouldn't know the truth if it jumped out of a pie and smacked you in the eye. You can't go making our feast gloomy with your tales of Greek victory," Helen hissed. She turned to the guards at the table. "Execute the liar!"

I turned. I ran. I tumbled down the hill to home. I shook my mother awake and dragged her to the secret gate and out onto the windy plain.

We rested among the rocks that night and slept among the sweet scent of flowers, and the sweeter scent of freedom.

We awoke to the sound of squealing wheels.

The wooden horse was being dragged through the great main gates of Troy.

ENDINGS

You know the rest of the tale, I guess. Once inside the city, the Greek soldiers climbed out of the wooden horse and opened the gates.

The Greek army returned, just as I'd said they would.

The rest was slaughter.

Paris and every man and boy were killed – except the one boy who was hiding in the hills, watching.

Every woman and girl was carried off as a slave to Greece. Helen was taken home to her husband.

The mighty city burned and fell. The walls cracked and crumbled in the heat.

Troy died that day.

We lived among the ruins for many years. My mother died in time, as mothers do.

That was a lifetime ago. There is only one Trojan left to tell the truth.

The Greek poets sing their side of the story. I am left to sing mine alone. The song is of 'The Boy Who Cried Horse'.

The trouble is, I told lies. But I'm not lying now.

As Aesop the Greek storyteller said, "There is no believing a liar, even when he speaks the truth."

You believe me, don't you? I am Acheron the Liar. The last Trojan.

And that was my story.

EPILOGUE

The Greek defeat of Troy is one of the oldest tales ever told. Some of it may be true, but a lot must have been made up. The wooden horse trick is a good story, but do you believe the people of Troy would be

stupid enough to take an enemy's gift into their city?

Some people say the tale may have a little bit of truth in it. The ruins of Troy have been discovered. However, it seems likely that the mighty walls were wrecked by an earthquake.

On the other hand, the Greek god of earthquakes is called Poseidon. In Greek pictures and statues, Poseidon looks like a horse. If Poseidon defeated Troy, and Poseidon was a horse, perhaps a horse really did defeat Troy!

YOU TRY

1. Word fun

In this story, Paris mixes up his words 'like wet washing on a windy day'. Can you play with words so they sound strange but still make some sense? Maybe you could take a nursery rhyme and move the words around. 'Mary had a little lamb' might look like this:

Little Lambie Mary had-o
Fleece it was as white as snow
Mary everywhere that went and
Lambie-little sure's to go.

Try it with 'Baa, Baa, Black Sheep' or 'Jack and Jill' – or any rhyme you know well.

2. I spy

The legend of Troy tells that a spy called Sinon went into the city to tell the Trojans about the wooden horse. This gave Sinon had a chance to look around the city. The Greeks

had never been inside the walls –
if they were going to jump out of
the wooden horse and attack, they
needed a map.

Imagine YOU are Sinon. Draw a
map of Troy and mark on it the six
most important places to attack.
There would be the palace (where
Paris and Helen lived) and the camp
(where the Trojan soldiers were
sleeping) – see if you can think
of four more. Remember to add
the mighty walls with their gates,
too – and the secret entrance that
Acheron and Sinon used.